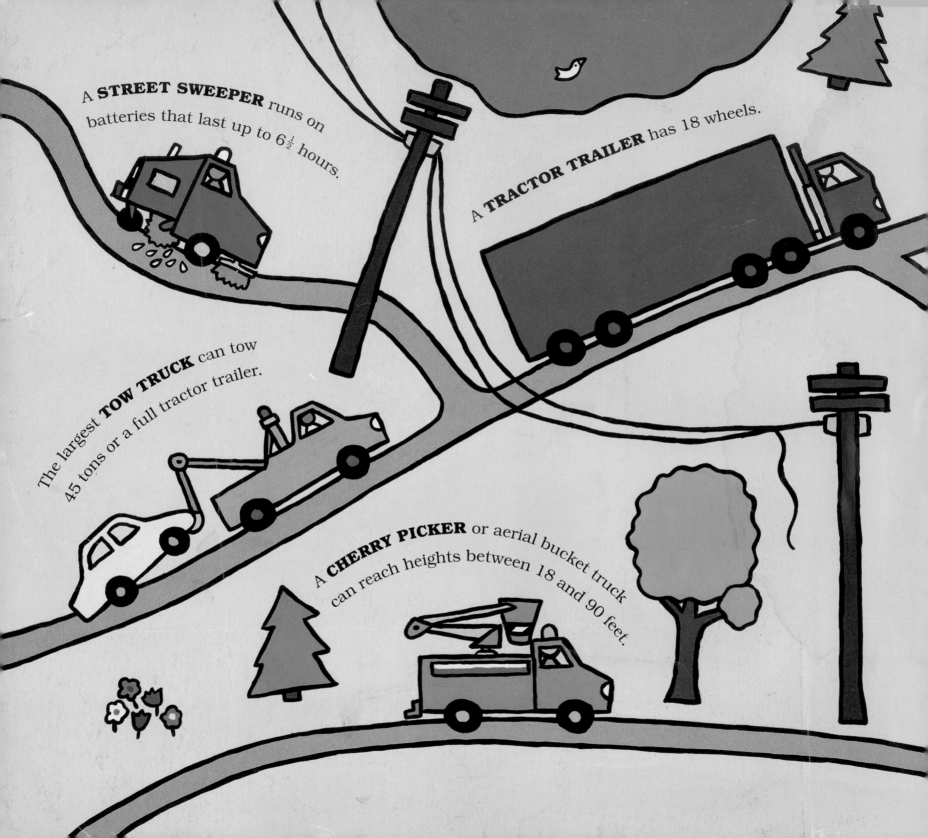

A **STREET SWEEPER** runs on batteries that last up to 6½ hours.

A **TRACTOR TRAILER** has 18 wheels.

The largest **TOW TRUCK** can tow 45 tons or a full tractor trailer.

A **CHERRY PICKER** or aerial bucket truck can reach heights between 18 and 90 feet.

A **FORKLIFT** can lift a load 23 feet into the air, or as high as the second story of a building.

A **GARBAGE TRUCK** weighs 25 tons, as much as five elephants.

The wheels of a **STEAMROLLER** are hollow and can be filled with sand or water to add weight.

A **BULLDOZER** would win a tug-of-war against 250 people.

*To Tractor Bob
and Betty*
—P.S.

For Paul
—S.H.

I LOVE TRUCKS!

Text copyright © 1999 by Philemon Sturges

Illustrations copyright © 1999 by Shari Halpern

Printed in the U.S.A. All rights reserved.

Library of Congress Cataloging-in-Publication Data

Sturges, Philemon.

I love trucks! / by Philemon Sturges ; illustrated by Shari Halpern.

p. cm. Summary: A child names many of his favorite trucks and each one's most notable characteristic.

ISBN 0-06-027819-6 — ISBN 0-06-443758-2 (pbk.)

1. Trucks—Juvenile literature. [1. Trucks.] I. Halpern, Shari, ill. II. Title.

TL230.15.S78 1999   97-29414   629.224—dc21   CIP   AC

Typography by Elynn Cohen and Christine Casarsa

Visit us on the World Wide Web! www.harperchildrens.com

I Love Trucks!

BY **PHILEMON STURGES**

ILLUSTRATED BY **SHARI HALPERN**

HarperCollins*Publishers*

Trucks, trucks, trucks! I like trucks.

Trailer trucks,

tow trucks,

trucks that sweep the street.

Trucks that crawl,

trucks that roll,

trucks that mix concrete.

This one digs.

This one dumps.

This one strings
up wires.

Some gobble trash.

Some lift up stuff.

This one zooms to fires!

I like trucks that blink and scream.

I like trucks that roar.

But the truck that I like best
brings ice cream to my door.

Trucks, trucks, trucks!
I LOVE trucks!

A **BACKHOE** can reach down to 20 feet, or as deep as the bottoms of some rivers.

A **POLICE TRUCK** often carries rescue equipment, such as inflatable boats and a giant airbag.

The largest **DUMP TRUCK** can hold 100 tons, or about 18 elephants.

The body of a **CEMENT MIXER** turns so that the dry cement mixes with water and is ready to use on arrival.

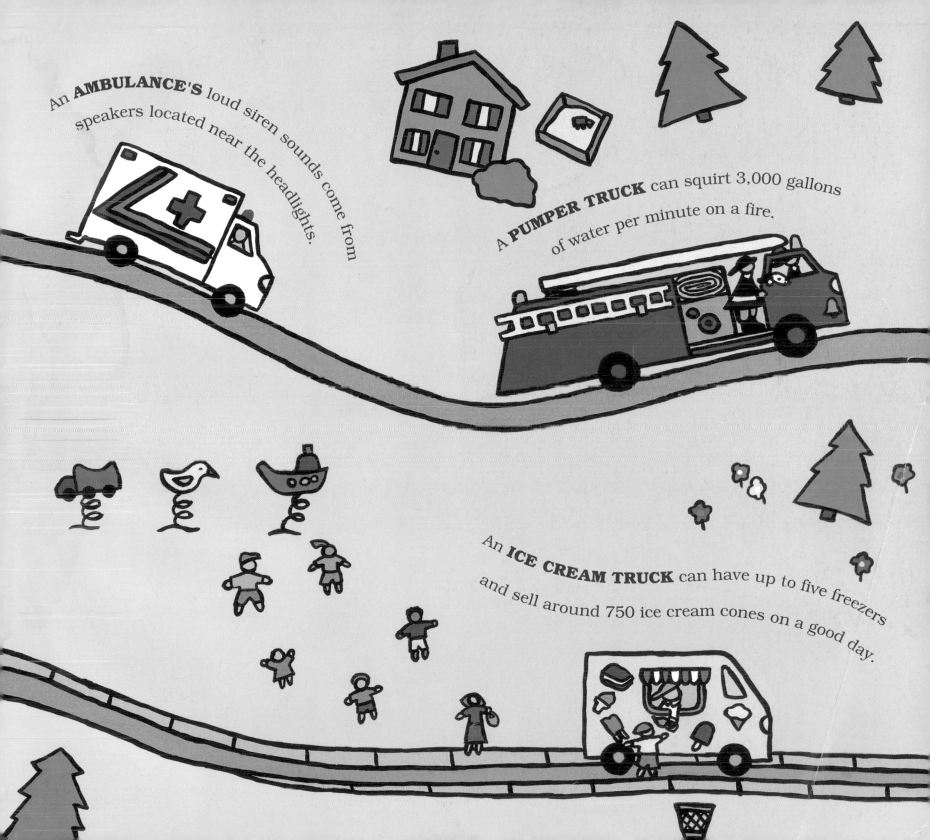

An **AMBULANCE'S** loud siren sounds come from speakers located near the headlights.

A **PUMPER TRUCK** can squirt 3,000 gallons of water per minute on a fire.

An **ICE CREAM TRUCK** can have up to five freezers and sell around 750 ice cream cones on a good day.